This book belongs to:

Editor: Tasha Percy
Designer: Rosie Levine
Editorial Director: Victoria Garrard
Art Director: Laura Roberts-Jensen

Copyright © QED Publishing 2015
A NEW BURLINGTON BOOK

First published in the UK in 2015 by QED Publishing
A Quarto Group company, The Old Brewery,
6 Blundell Street, London, N7 9BH

www.qed-publishing.co.uk

A catalogue record for this book is available from the British Library.

ISBN 978 1 78493 044 8

Printed in China

The lion who lost his ROAR,
but learnt to draw

Paula Knight and
Daniel Howarth

NEW
BURLINGTON
BOOKS

"RRRRRROAR!"

Lionel loved to roar.

He had a **deafening** voice.

It **startled** butterflies and birds and **scattered** herds of animals.

"Please can you **try** to be a little quieter, Lionel?" asked Papa. "You've disturbed the birds, flustered the butterflies and the zebras are hiding again!"

"RRRRROAR!"

"You're giving me a headache!" said Mama.
"Why don't you sit quietly and draw?"

"Drawing is **boring**! I like
RRRROARING!"

So Lionel did just that – all day long.
Lionel's roar drowned out the
whoosh of the waterfall.

He **shocked** a
flock of flamingos.

He **alarmed**
the aardvarks.

He **panicked**
the parrots.

Next morning, Lionel tiptoed
to Mama and Papa's bed.

He opened his mouth...

But nothing happened!

His ROAR was no more.

"Oh dear!" Mama said.

"All that roaring
has made your
throat sore!"

Lionel was thirsty. He pointed to his mouth.
"I don't know what you mean," said Papa.

Lionel went to the lake for a drink.

The flock of flamingos **squawked** at him, but Lionel couldn't speak.

The parrots on their
perches said "**Crawk**"
but Lionel couldn't reply.

The monkeys **chattered**,
but Lionel was silent.

The elephants **trumpeted**,
but Lionel could only sigh.

"Look Lionel,"
said Monkey,
"you've drawn a pattern!"

"It's a curly swirl – just like my tail!"

"Drawn?" thought Lionel.
"But drawing's **boring**!"

"Pretty pattern, pretty pattern!" squawked the parrots.

Lionel had to agree that the pattern did look rather good.

"Can you draw me?" asked Flamingo.

"And me?" added Monkey.

Lionel could only nod.

He bounded home, and the
other animals followed him.

He chose a pink crayon, and started to scribble.

When Lionel handed over his drawing, Flamingo was **SO** happy.

"Thank you, Lionel. It looks just like me!"

Drawing was **fun!**

The different coloured crayons matched the things around him:

Bright blue

Pretty pink

Glossy green

Yummy yellow

"How lovely," said Mama.
"You do like drawing, after all!"

"N...n...o," Lionel croaked.

His voice was coming back.

" I...like...

Drrrrrroaaaarring!"

Next steps

Show the children the cover again. By looking at the cover, could they have guessed what Lionel would do in the story?

In the story, Lionel is reluctant to try something new. Can the children think of anything new that they would like to try? Why do they think he doesn't like drawing at first?

The jungle animals are sick of Lionel's noisy roaring in the story. Discuss with the children when it is not a good idea to make lots of noise, and when it's acceptable to be noisy. Do the children think that Lionel will be less noisy now that he can draw?

Let the children draw their favourite animals, and ask them what colours they have chosen. Ideally, make a range of materials available for them to use.

Lionel used his tail to draw with at first. Discuss how other animals might use different parts of their bodies to draw with. For example, an elephant might use its trunk.

Do the children think drawing is fun? Tell them that anyone of any age can draw, and ask them what is their favourite thing to draw. Why do they enjoy drawing?